BIONICLE

DARK
HUNTERS

b

Dark hunters
JSF Far   39092001038852

Silver City Public Library

DATE DUE

SILVER CITY PUBL
SILVER CITY, N

D0388466

SCHOLASTIC INC.

NEW YORK   TORONTO   LONDON   AUCKLAND   SYDNEY

MEXICO CITY   NEW DELHI   HONG KONG   BU

JSF
Far 0273092 1/17 $7⁰⁰

*For Toby, Adam, Steve, Jeremy, Christian, Carlos,
Randy, and Stuart, whose artistic talents help
bring BIONICLE to life.*—Greg

No part of this publication may be reproduced in whole or in part, stored
in a retrieval system, or transmitted in any form or by any means,
electronic, mechanical, photocopying, recording, or otherwise,
without written permission of the publisher. For information
regarding permission, write to Scholastic Inc., Attention:
Permissions Department, 557 Broadway, New York, NY 10012.

ISBN 0-439-82803-1

LEGO, the LEGO logo and BIONICLE are trademarks
of the LEGO Group and used here by special permission.
© 2006 The LEGO Group.

All rights reserved. Published by Scholastic Inc.
SCHOLASTIC and associated logos are trademarks
and/or registered trademarks of Scholastic Inc.

12 11 10 9 8 7 6 5 4 3 2 1   6 7 8 9 10/0

Printed in the U.S.A.
First printing, June 2006

The Dark Hunters — for thousands of years, that name has brought fear to the hearts of everyone from Toa heroes to Matoran to members of the Brotherhood of Makuta itself. Gathered from every corner of the universe, these thieves, enforcers, and monstrosities have come together in an organization whose reach extends into every council chamber and every shadowy corner.

I, the Shadowed One, brought these warriors and wanderers together. For the right price, they will do anything, regardless of the danger. Those of them who are wise have learned to fear my wrath far more than any other consequence of their deeds. My Dark Hunters have stolen artifacts worth more than the whole of Metru Nui; they've made Turaga simply vanish into the night; they've spied, deceived, and brought destruction to countless lands — all in the name of profit and power.

In this volume, I have collected information on some of my most valued and effective Dark Hunters. Each has been assigned a unique (and false) name, in the event this collection should fall into the hands of Toa or some other self-appointed guardian of light. The sole exceptions are those Dark Hunters who do not leave my side, those who are no more, and those few who have become rogue. And, of course, there are some I have omitted from this record, for their current missions are such that even speaking their names aloud could bring risk of exposure.

I do not expect that anyone other than myself will ever read this. But if I am wrong, and someone else sets eyes upon it — well, I would advise that you remain in the light and stay close to whatever friends you may have. For the Dark Hunters are no doubt already seeking you out . . . and you won't like what happens when they find you.

— The Shadowed One

THE SHADOWED ONE

Any collection of Dark Hunters must begin with me, the founder and ruler of this organization. My true name has been lost to history, and it is doubtful anyone remembers it besides myself . . . and if they do, they would not dare to speak it aloud.

Since no one other than I will ever read this volume, I will detail some of my personal history here. I come from a land of shadows and ice, a place that was never "blessed" by the loving gaze of Mata Nui. When the Matoran were granted their special status, when the Brotherhood of Makuta came to serve Mata Nui's will, those who dwelled in my land were ignored and abandoned. Determined to carve out an empire for myself, I began taking on the tasks Matoran were too timid to do and the Brotherhood saw as beneath it.

Now, centuries later, I lead hundreds of Dark Hunters scattered throughout the known universe. From my fortress, I assign them their missions, house the treasure they collect, and enforce our laws. Disobedience is met with extermination. Treachery is met with far worse . . . for traitors are not granted the mercy of death.

POWERS: In addition to my formidable strength, I possess eyebeams capable of disintegrating virtually any substance. My staff can be used to create solid protodermis strong enough to imprison a Toa. I have suffered only one defeat in combat, at the hands of Makuta, for which I will someday be avenged.

STATUS: Active. Despite my unnaturally advanced age (the result of a battle with Makuta), I remain in firm control of the Dark Hunters. Only the Piraka have dared to challenge my rule, and they will pay dearly for that.

AIRWATCHER

Airwatcher serves as one of many sentries protecting the island of the Dark Hunters. Why, given his formidable powers, do I not send him on missions? Simply put, he makes Krekka look like a genius of the highest level. His stupidity makes him easy to manipulate, but also less than useful as an operative.

A pair of Dark Hunters went to Airwatcher's native land on a mission, only to find themselves attacked by this fierce being. One was killed. The other captured Airwatcher and brought him back to me. I rapidly convinced Airwatcher that working for me was far better than the alternative and dispatched him to the northern mountains to patrol.

How effective is he? Ah, there is no way to know. You see, there is rarely anything left of any intruder foolish enough to encounter Airwatcher.

POWERS: Airwatcher's wings allow him to fly for short distances. His chest-mounted launchers project energy webs that bind a target. His staff then fires a stream of acid to disintegrate the unfortunate. Airwatcher normally strikes from high above, and he has been known, on occasion, to capture and dispatch rocks, trees, and other Dark Hunters who have wandered into his patrol zone.

STATUS: Active. Yes, he's an idiot, but he's a useful idiot. He has been trained not to attack me or Sentrakh, and so we can travel to his area and hide items of importance there. It is one of the few places on the island we know no other Dark Hunter will dare go, given Airwatcher's quick temper and acidic approach to problems.

DESIGNED BY ADRIEN PERINET

AMPHIBAX

Few outsiders could describe Amphibax, for few have ever seen him and lived. This sleek amphibious being is my first choice for all underwater operations, combining the cunning of a natural predator, the cold, calculating intelligence of a thief, and the savagery of a Takea shark.

Prior to joining the Dark Hunters, Amphibax was a wanderer beneath the waves. His missing hand would seem to indicate he lost at least one battle during this time. Why he was forced to live this way remains a mystery — perhaps he was exiled by some undersea land that tired of his brutality. Regardless, he found his way into the ranks of Dark Hunters.

Now he serves me, striking at Brotherhood of Makuta vessels and raiding the coastlines of Matoran islands at my command. Even the rumor that he is in the area is enough to bring all seagoing traffic to a halt. In some ways, his reputation is almost as formidable a weapon as his claws.

POWERS: Amphibax has long, sharp claws on one hand and a spiny whip in place of the other. He is an extremely powerful swimmer and able to survive at great depths for an extended period of time. On land, he is a swift runner and a powerful tree climber. He has heightened senses of hearing and sight.

STATUS: Active. Amphibax is currently off the coast of Voya Nui, keeping track of events there.

DESIGNED BY WILLY REESE

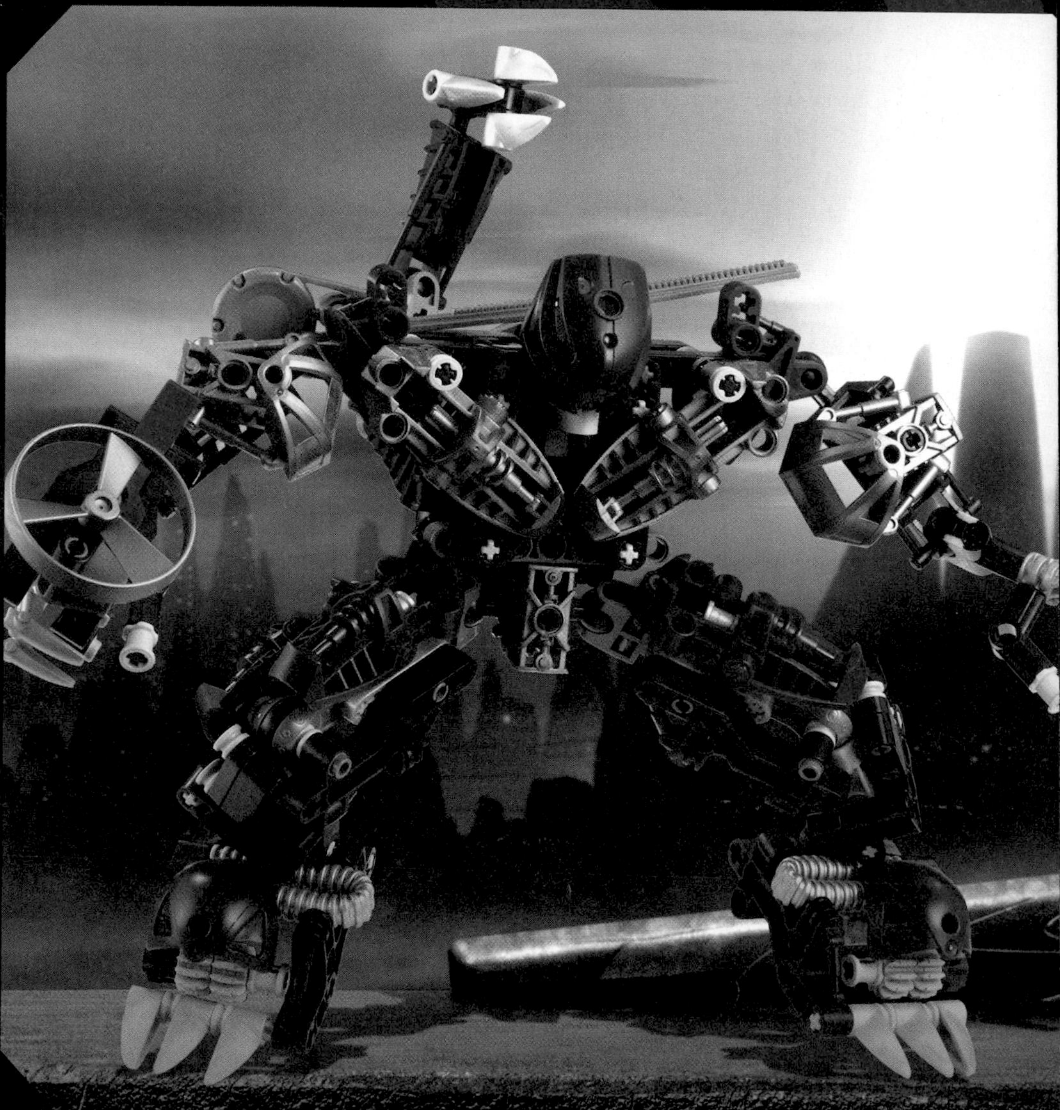

ANCIENT

Ancient may be the only Dark Hunter who is older than I. He was, in fact, the inspiration for my creation of this organization. Now he works for me and is, after Sentrakh, my most trusted operative.

A native of my home island, Ancient rebelled against the strict codes of behavior imposed on us and carved out a new life for himself. He began hiring himself out to whoever could pay and, in the process, transformed what had been a dull, peaceful society into a fragmented land dominated by warlords. Each competed with the others for Ancient's services, and he repaid his employers by ruthlessly crushing their enemies. He had no conscience and no reluctance about switching sides on a moment's notice if he got a better offer.

I encountered him toward the end of the civil war and recognized the wisdom in his actions. He agreed with me that there existed a demand in the world at large for beings willing to do anything for a price. And with that, the idea that eventually evolved into the Dark Hunters was born.

POWERS: Ancient is possessed of great strength and powerful armor that is impenetrable to most physical attacks. His boots are fitted with levitation disks, activated by stamping on the ground, which enable him to rise into the air. He carries an upgraded Rhotuka launcher capable of rapid fire. His Rhotuka spinners rob a foe of all physical coordination.

STATUS: Active. Despite his advanced age, Ancient remains an effective enforcer and "launcher for hire." He is currently teamed with Voporak in a search for the Mask of Time.

DESIGNED BY CONNOR HARVEY

AVAK

A short time ago, seven Dark Hunters dared to abandon the order and strike out on their own in a bid for power. Six of these are detailed in this journal — the seventh has had his entry torn out and burned. Avak is one of these, an ambitious, discontented tinkerer who will find it difficult to work after I have his hands removed.

Avak was originally the target of a Dark Hunter mission. One of our number had been captured and imprisoned, and Avak was the jailer. What we did not know at the time was that the prison cell had been conjured by Avak's mind. When he was defeated, the cell faded away. Seeing the potential benefits of such a power, the Dark Hunters brought Avak back to my island.

Almost immediately, he was a problem. Complaining, questioning authority, scheming against his betters . . . all of this earned him his share of dangerous missions and a number of sessions with the masters of pain. Somehow, he survived all of it, only to betray the Dark Hunters and embark on a quest to find the Mask of Life. Eventually, my shadow will fall on this Piraka again, and he will find that his power is no match for mine.

POWERS: Avak has the ability to create from thin air a prison capable of holding any being. He is also extremely skilled at crafting equipment and weapons. His X-ray and telescopic vision make it easy for him to put things together or take them apart. He carries a zamor sphere launcher and a dual weapon with pick axe on one end and jackhammer on the other.

STATUS: Rogue. Avak is currently on the island of Voya Nui with five other traitors. They call themselves Piraka. . . . I call them doomed.

CHARGER

Certainly one of the most unusual Dark Hunters, Charger began his life as a Kane-Ra bull, of all things. Now he thinks and speaks like any other member of my organization, though he smells far worse. Just how he transformed from a grazing Rahi to a hardened hunter remains a mystery, but there is no doubting his effectiveness in his new role.

It must be remembered that Kane-Ra are brave and bold to the point of being unstoppable and well near suicidal. Put a wall in front of them, they go through it. . . . Put a canyon before them, they try to jump it. . . . And the same applies to Charger. I never send him on a mission that involves fighting less than six foes, all of them more powerful than he. Inevitably, he is still standing and they are strewn around the ground like broken Kanohi masks.

Of course, he is not without his weak points. He reacts violently to the presence of other Rahi, particularly Muaka. He is the furthest thing from a strategic thinker, and he is not particularly skilled at stealth. Send him to steal an object from a citadel and he will first bring down the fortress, then retrieve the item from the rubble. But as long as his approach works, I am willing to ignore his methods . . . and his smell.

POWERS: Sharp blades wielded by a brutally strong Dark Hunter — what could be more satisfying? Charger also carries an axe looted from a Toa long ago, capable of absorbing elemental energy and hurling it back at a foe.

STATUS: Active. He is currently tracking down some Matoran laborers who evidently tired of the hospitality of my island. Perhaps he will even bring them back in one piece this time. . . .

DESIGNED BY THANE RATLIFF

CONJURER

The being I call Conjurer was the warrior-king of a land far
to the south of Voya Nui. He gained and held power thanks
to sophisticated technology that enabled him to perform
feats that seemed almost magical to his Matoran subjects.
Although he relished his power and his reign, he was unable
to expand his kingdom (Matoran make notoriously poor
conquering armies). So when he was presented with the
opportunity to add to his power and wealth by becoming a
Dark Hunter, he leapt at the chance.

Despite the fact that I know his powers can all be explained
away, he maintains his image as a mysterious loner in touch
with forces beyond anyone else's understanding. He goes out
of his way to carry out his missions with a dramatic flair that
leaves witnesses wondering just how he managed to
accomplish his great feats. And all the while, he schemes to
take over the Dark Hunters, never realizing that my
"magic" is more powerful than his by far.

POWERS: Conjurer has powerful telekinetic abilities and
carries a staff of disintegration (although he claims the
power belongs to him, not the staff). His Kanoka disks can
temporarily steal the power of an opponent and channel it
to Conjurer. He has an intense hatred of water, though the
reason why has not yet been discovered.

STATUS: Temporarily inactive. Conjurer attempted to
absorb the power of a member of the Brotherhood of
Makuta and overloaded his own system in the process.
When he awakens . . . *if* he awakens . . . he may perhaps have
learned humility.

DESIGNED BY STEPHEN RAMBERG

DARKNESS

Every ruler must have a shadow, a being who watches and waits every moment of the day. At the first sign of weakness, the shadow pounces, defeats the ruler, and assumes the throne for himself. It is a brutal but necessary way to make sure that compassion and doubt never enter a ruler's heart. Darkness is my shadow, perched high above my throne, waiting for me to slip just once.

He is silent as he watches. No one, not even I, knows what goes on behind his bloodred eyes. Now and then, he descends to discipline an incompetent Dark Hunter just to keep in practice. Then he returns as he came, his gaze fixed ever upon me. He leaves the island only when I do, somehow managing to keep me in sight even when he does not travel with me.

Could I defeat Darkness in a fair battle? My answer must be no, but not because he is more powerful or more cunning than I. The reason is that on the day when I hesitate, or fail to strike ruthlessly at a foe, I will have already lost the edge needed to crush my shadow.

POWERS: Unknown. I have seen him rend a foe with his claws, and I have seen him bend and slither through places too narrow for any being to pass into. But are those the limit of his powers? I doubt that very much.

STATUS: Active. He watches me even now.

DESIGNED BY RICHARD GLOVER

DWELLER

Although one might not guess it from his appearance, Dweller has one of the most important jobs in the entire Dark Hunter organization. He is on permanent assignment to the city of Metru Nui, tasked with monitoring what goes on there and relaying the information to me via messages attached to Rahi. That city is strategically vital to both the Brotherhood of Makuta and the Dark Hunters, and recent events suggest it may soon be a prime time to take it.

At first glance, Dweller's raw strength is obvious. But his true powers lie in his mind, and these are what have made him so valuable. From his post in the Archives, he has been able to keep track of all that goes on in the city, as well as screen himself from the Rahaga and others who have wandered through the catacombs beneath Metru Nui. He is smart, he is silent, and he is patient, having already spent close to 1,000 years on this post.

His most recent dispatch indicates that only Toa Takanuva remains to guard the city. This may be the moment for Dweller to take a more active role, strike at the Matoran, and prepare the city for seizure by my forces.

POWERS: From his home far beneath Onu-Metru, Dweller can reach out with his mind and probe the thoughts of others or drive them mad with nightmares. He is also able to screen himself from others' perceptions so he cannot be spotted.

STATUS: Active. His current mission is to track Toa Takanuva and strike at him when the Toa of Light is at his most distracted.

ELIMINATOR

Eliminator was the third of three Dark Hunters hired by Makuta during his failed attempt to seize control of Metru Nui and its Matoran population. While the other two were in the city acting as close support, Eliminator's job was to track down and defeat the city's Toa guardians. Makuta, disguised as the city elder, had ordered them on missions outside of Metru Nui, making them easy targets for my Dark Hunter.

That was long ago. Today, Eliminator acts as a troubleshooter of sorts for my organization. If a Dark Hunter fails in his mission, Eliminator is dispatched. His first task is to annihilate the incompetent who could not complete the task. His second is to carry the mission to conclusion himself. At both of these, he excels.

Eliminator is universally hated by his fellow Dark Hunters and rarely returns to my island base. Despite his sheer power, there is always the possibility that his comrades might join together in an effort to eliminate him.

POWERS: Eliminator has the ability to harness and combine the powers of up to four Kanoka disks, projecting the resultant energies from his razor-sharp talons in lightning-like bursts. He can also hurl Kanoka disks from his back-mounted launchers. He is agile and swift, despite his size. Shadows seem to cling to him, making him nearly invisible in low-light conditions.

STATUS: Active. Eliminator is currently on another island, waiting for one of his fellow Dark Hunters to commit the unforgivable sin of failure.

DESIGNED BY ROB DRABKOWSKI

FIREDRACAX

One of our more recent recruits, Firedracax is unusual in that he is not fueled by a hatred of Toa, greed, or a lust for power. He joined the Dark Hunters for one reason only: to kill Visorak.

At one time, he was an ordinary Matoran, living on an idyllic little island well to the south of Metru Nui. His peaceful life was shattered when the Visorak invaded. Panicked, he and some of his friends fled, only to fall into a pool of energized protodermis. All but one perished . . . and that one was transformed into an armored titan with a bitter hatred of Makuta's little army of spiders.

Needless to say, being at war with the Brotherhood of Makuta, the Dark Hunters were more than willing to take Firedracax in. Although the Visorak are now scattered and leaderless, he is still quick to hunt them down. I allow him to do so, for there is no good reason to allow Makuta to have a potential legion to raise against me.

POWERS: Firedracax is equipped with an unbreakable shield. His Rhotuka spinner absorbs all thermal energy from the air and directs it at a foe as a devastating blast of heat and flame.

STATUS: Active. I recently dispatched him to an island where there is reportedly a colony of Visorak. Of course, he may also run into some of the Brotherhood of Makuta's operatives there as well, which will be too bad . . . for them.

DESIGNED BY MICHAEL STEIGER

GATHERER

Many beings are drawn to the life of a Dark Hunter by the potential for profit and adventure, or simply to escape the life they have been living before. Others, like Gatherer, were pulled into the organization by force and given no choice about remaining.

In his former life, Gatherer was a Matoran — a leader among Matoran, in fact, renowned for his honesty, fairness, and all those other contemptible virtues. When he became an obstacle to Dark Hunter operations in the area, I ordered his capture. After a bit of . . . persuasion, he was made to see things my way. Now he works for me, using the powers I gave him to hunt down my enemies. With each successful mission, he takes a piece of armor from his opponent and adds it to his own, becoming the colossus you see today.

Does he, at times, miss his old life? Does some part of him rebel against his existence as a Dark Hunter, and long for the innocence of a Matoran? I don't know. I don't care. He will continue to carry out his missions as ordered, or else someone, someday, will be collecting pieces of his armor as trophies of a kill.

POWERS: Gatherer has been engineered so that he has no need of food or sleep. He has a psychic connection to Rahi who dwell underground and can command them to do his bidding. He also carries a wide array of weapons, including one blade that can slice through solid protodermis, another that doubles as a shield, and an energy cannon. His Rhotuka spinner carries the *mind scramble* power.

STATUS: Active. Gatherer last reported that he is on the trail of a mysterious third player in this game, someone besides the Dark Hunters and the Brotherhood of Makuta, who claims power in this universe. I anxiously await his findings.

DESIGNED BY SAM WINFIELD

GLADIATOR

There are some cultures that thrive on war. One such was the island home of Sidorak and Krekka, a place where battle was a constant fact of life. Even their entertainment was built around violence, as massive warriors fought to the death in an arena for the amusement of their betters. The Dark Hunter I have named Gladiator was one such.

He had always been a crowd favorite, beating native opponents and prisoners from other islands. One night, during a particularly fierce battle, he lost control and went on a rampage. At least a dozen of Krekka's species were summoned to bring him down, but he demolished them all. It took half a precinct's worth of guards to finally stop him.

His power and skill had attracted the attention of one of my Dark Hunters. On his own initiative, that Hunter broke Gladiator out of prison and transported him to my island. Although at first difficult to control, his hunger for battle outweighed his hatred of authority, and he became another weapon in my arsenal.

POWERS: Gladiator's primary power is his brute strength, backed up by vicious claws and an incredible resistance to damage. Often, his presence alone is so intimidating that he does not even need to strike a blow to achieve his goals.

STATUS: Active. He is currently back in the arena on his native island, this time as my spy, investigating rumors that the late Sidorak's people are trying to reassemble the Visorak horde.

DESIGNED BY NATHANIEL AND ZACHARY SAGER

GUARDIAN

Guardian is the keeper of secrets. He stays on the periphery of any major conflict between the Dark Hunters and major foes like the Toa or the Brotherhood of Makuta. His task is a simple one: If a Dark Hunter is captured, it is his job to silence him before any secrets can be divulged to our enemies.

This Dark Hunter originally came from an island wracked by war. His tribe had been betrayed by one of their own and delivered into the hands of their enemies. Guardian was injured in a Rhotuka spinner crossfire and left for dead. One of my Dark Hunters stumbled upon him and, seeing a potential ally, restored him to health.

Once on my island, he was outfitted with new weapons and given a new purpose. He who had been betrayed by a comrade would live to ensure that no Dark Hunter would ever get the chance to commit such treachery. Fueled by rage and a desire for revenge, he has proven to be ruthlessly effective at silencing possible defectors.

POWERS: Guardian's right arm was rebuilt to allow him to wield a staff that launches Rhotuka spinners. His spinners contain powers tied to stone and earth. For up-close and personal dealings, his claws are more than sufficient.

STATUS: Active. Guardian has been kept extremely busy by the Dark Hunters–Brotherhood of Makuta war, and I expect it will be some time before he will know any rest.

DESIGNED BY JORDAN STEELQUIST

HAKANN

Having Hakann as an ally is like . . . having a Doom Viper curled up next to you at night. In a line of work that considers the ability to betray a virtue, Hakann has become the master of the double and triple cross. Some of his former colleagues said you could not turn your back on him. The truth is, he would happily look you right in the eyes while stabbing you in the back.

Hakann is one of the seven who defected from my organization and became Piraka. Were it not for him, I would have no idea where they were or what they were seeking. But even as they made their way to the island of Voya Nui, Hakann sent a message to me through one of my agents, telling me the outline of their plan and their destination. Why? To hasten the elimination of his companions, of course, and to gain favor with me just in case their little rebellion failed.

Each and every Piraka is powerful, ruthless, thoroughly selfish, and possibly mad. But they have no idea what they did when they let Hakann join their ranks. He will be the death of them all — unless I beat him to that honor.

POWERS: Hakann can generate devastating bolts of mental energy as well as blasts of heat vision. He carries a dual-use weapon with a claw on one side and a lava launcher on the other, along with a zamor sphere launcher.

STATUS: Rogue. If things go bad on Voya Nui, Hakann will attempt to return to the Dark Hunters. We will be waiting to welcome him, in our own special way.

HORDIKA DRAGONS

Unlike most of the Dark Hunters included in this tome, the Hordika Dragons are not one individual, but eight. Some time ago, a small group of Visorak spiders were unwise enough to come to my island. I had them captured and their venom analyzed. It seemed quite an amazing substance, and I was anxious to see just what it could do. And so I selected eight of my Dark Hunters and had them exposed to it.

The result was the lizardlike beasts you see here. Savage, violent, vicious, and treacherous, they have proven to be a discipline problem since their creation. But their fearsome aspect does have its uses.

Of course, at some point, their Hordika side will take over completely and they will be good for little more than particularly brutal house pets. But until that day, I find them most helpful in collecting on debts from clients who are reluctant to pay.

POWERS: In addition to enhanced strength, agility, and tracking sense, the Hordika Dragons have a natural electric charge that flows through their claws. This power can be turned on and off at will, and allows them to electrocute anything they touch.

STATUS: Active. It is sad to think that so many beings refuse to abide by their agreements and attempt to withhold pay, forcing me to use the Hordika Dragons to get it. What has happened to honor in this universe?

DESIGNED BY AUSTIN STOEFFLER

KRAATA-KAL

Anyone who has had occasion to war with the Brotherhood of Makuta (as I have) knows the Rahkshi all too well. Makuta pulls a serpentlike creature called a kraata from his substance, exposes it to energized protodermis, and then it transforms into Rahkshi armor. But the Rahkshi were not the limit of what kraata could become, and Kraata-Kal is proof of that.

Makuta exposed a kraata to a mixture of the same energies used to mutate Bohrok into Bohrok-Kal. The result was a vastly intelligent and powerful serpent with control over fire, water, and shadow. Makuta constructed a suit of armor far more powerful than that of a Rahkshi to house his new creation. The armor itself was an offensive weapon, fitted with "claws" and "teeth" to ward off attackers.

Kraata-Kal is extremely ambitious and has, on more than one occasion, ignored his mission objectives in the interests of his own profit. The last time this happened, I had Vezok show him how easily armor can be shattered when you know how.

POWERS: In addition to the powers mentioned above, Kraata-Kal carries a double-bladed flame sword and a Kanoka disk launcher.

STATUS: Active. He has just completed his recovery from wounds suffered in a fight with other Dark Hunters and is part of a team being assembled to capture the Piraka.

DESIGNED BY MORGAN ALFREJO

KREKKA & NIDHIKI

An almost perfect team . . . the sheer, raw, brute strength of Krekka paired with the cunning and craftiness of Nidhiki. The latter was a reluctant Dark Hunter, always looking for some way to escape the life, and the former a mindless mass of muscle who made sure Nidhiki followed orders.

Krekka was living a simple, violent life as a guard on his home island, until he interfered with a representative of the Brotherhood of Makuta. He lost his job, along with one of his eyes, and was forced to flee his home. He eventually broke enough opponents in two to attract the attention of one of my Dark Hunters and was recruited to join the organization.

Nidhiki was originally a Toa of Air. Disgraced after a failed attempt to betray the city of Metru Nui into my hands, he was banished from that wretched place and found refuge on my island. I dispatched him on minor assignments, always with Krekka as a partner, since the big, stupid brute was too blindly loyal to me to ever tolerate Nidhiki's attempts at betrayal. Eventually, Nidhiki attempted to buy passage off the island from a visiting stranger, Roodaka, and she repaid him by mutating him into a montrous, spiderlike form. Too hideous to be welcomed anywhere else, he was now forced to be a Dark Hunter forever.

POWERS: Krekka was enormously strong, well beyond the level of a Toa. He was capable of flight and could cast energy nets to trap a foe. His lack of speed and agility were more than made up for by his talent for rearranging body parts. Nidhiki was capable of flight, spitting force bolts at opponents, and planning ingenious ambushes.

STATUS: Dead. I sent them to aid Makuta in his attempt to seize control of Metru Nui. When it seemed as if his plans might be frustrated by Toa, he killed my two Dark Hunters, an event which prompted the centuries-long war between us and the Brotherhood of Makuta.

LURKER

Lurker comes from one of those backward islands where they still consider petty crimes like murder to be cause for banishment. Rather than strike back at his former neighbors, Lurker struck out on his own. He accepted any job he could get, some of which would have otherwise gone to Dark Hunters. Since I frown on competition, I recruited him.

Given an option as to what type of improvements he wanted, Lurker rejected weapons in favor of good old-fashioned equipment — stingers, blades, and claws. As an extra touch, he had two Kanohi mounted on his shoulders, intending them to look like trophies of combat.

Already agile and strong, his clawed arms made him an excellent climber. Toa have learned to look to the sky, just in case Lurker should drop down on them. Most recently, he made an example of a few bothersome Turaga, ensuring that their Matoran will keep quiet and continue to pay for our protection.

POWERS: Lurker is a natural hunter and fighter, with skills honed by years of surviving on his own. His new "natural" tools make it impossible for an opponent to know just where the next attack is coming from.

STATUS: Unknown. Lurker was sent to investigate rumors that Makuta had been killed by Toa. He has yet to return.

DESIGNED BY THOMAS DOLAN

LURKER

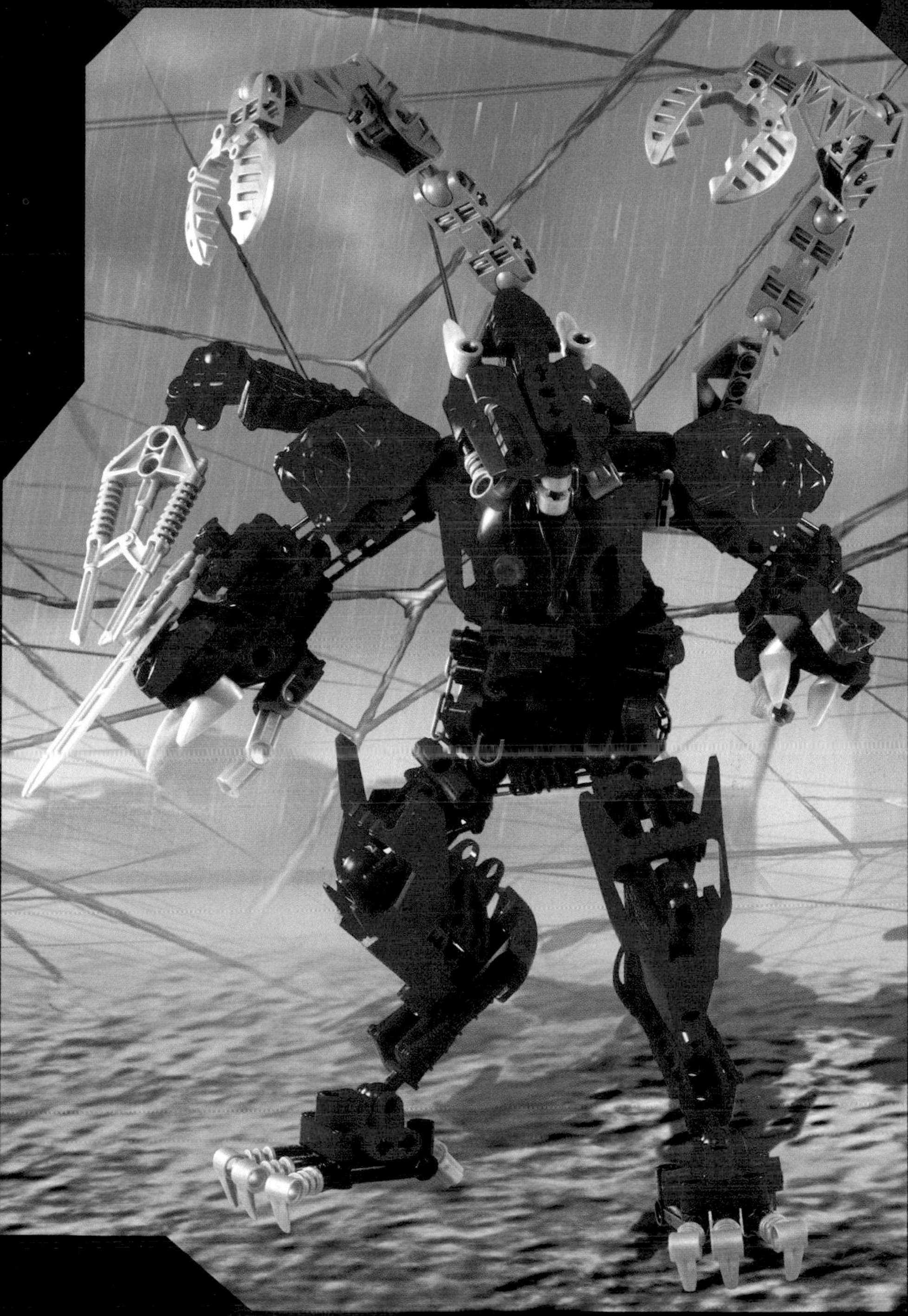

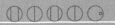

mimic

There is nothing quite as magical as friendship, or so I have been told. It can make one being risk everything and take foolish chances with little hope for reward. It can also make someone incredibly easy to manipulate.

Mimic is an example of the latter. He spent most of his life in the company of a friend from his native island. Their home had suffered a natural disaster and the two had worked together to survive. Along the way, Mimic discovered he had photographic reflexes and could duplicate any physical feat he saw, perfectly and without any practice. Shortly after learning this, his friend mysteriously disappeared.

Desperate to find her, Mimic began a long and fruitless search. It was easy to convince him that, in return for his services, I would put my Dark Hunters to work trying to find her. He has proven to be an effective operative, and will remain so as long as his friend remains missing. And so she shall for a very, very long time, for no one but Sentrakh and I know she is in one of the many dungeons beneath my fortress. As I said, friendship makes one so easy to fool.

POWERS: Show Mimic a being skilled at marksmanship, and he will become the perfect marksman. Let him watch a Dark Hunter skilled at swordplay for even a few seconds, and Mimic is a master of the sword. Were he to use his skills for his own benefit, he would be a power to reckon with in this universe. But his only thoughts are for his lost friend, and that is how I intend to keep it.

STATUS: Active. Mimic is assigned to missions far from my island and rarely allowed to return. Why risk his making the disturbing discovery of where his friend has been all this time?

DESIGNED BY KURTIS SPLETTER

minion

A potentially valuable pawn in my war with the Brotherhood of Makuta, Minion is reputed to have been an enforcer for the Brotherhood. Created during one of their many imaginative experiments with Rahi, Minion spent a great deal of time around Makuta and other members of his foul little group.

What none of the Brotherhood realized was that their experiments had increased Minion's intelligence to the point where he understood everything they were saying. He listened and he learned, planning to put his newfound knowledge to use someday. When the Toa Hagah rebelled against the Brotherhood, Minion took advantage of the confusion to escape and make his way to my island.

From that day to this, he has not spoken a word. I do not know if he was rendered mute by the Brotherhood's work or is simply keeping his secrets, but I have no doubt a wealth of knowledge is hidden in his bestial brain. Someday, I must find a way to extract it . . . even if the brain must come with it.

POWERS: Minion's hide is covered with impenetrable armor, and his claws are long and razor sharp. His tracking skills are such that he can sense the approach of a Brotherhood of Makuta member from a continent away.

STATUS: Active. I prefer to keep Minion close by, in case he suddenly finds his tongue. He also proves a most effective "watch-Rahi" against the unlikely event the Brotherhood attempts to attack my fortress.

DESIGNED BY JOHN BRODEUR

POISON

No, he is not the brightest mask in the storehouse, but Poison does have his uses to the Dark Hunters. For one, he has a ferocious hatred of Matoran, arising from the fact that his species was hunted to near extinction by the little fools. For another, he exhibits unquestioning loyalty to me. After all, thoughts of rebellion require a brain, do they not?

When my Dark Hunters first encountered Poison, he was making futile attacks against a Matoran settlement and being thoroughly thrashed by the local Toa. It was only after he had been brought to my island that we discovered he had not been using his primary offensive weapon: the poison that courses through his body. Nidhiki taught him how to put his venom to use, and also made a rather bizarre discovery — Poison's only real vulnerability is to his own venom!

Biologically, my researchers are unsure how this is possible. But it does afford Poison a certain amount of protection, for the only way his foes get access to his poison is when he infects them with it. And by then, it is too late to use it against him. . . .

POWERS: Poison is able to spit a paralyzing venom at his foes. It is inevitably fatal if left untreated for more than half an hour. He is also able to deliver a powerful stun with his tail.

STATUS: Active. His resemblance to pure Rahi causes most Toa to overlook him, not realizing that he is in fact a semi-intelligent being and a Dark Hunter.

DESIGNED BY ISAAC EVAVOLD

PRIMAL

Every now and then, there is a Dark Hunter who is almost more trouble than he is worth. Too annoying to retain, too efficient to kill . . . a perplexing problem.

Primal was a warrior from a savage tribe whose land was overrun by the Visorak. He led a small band of survivors in successful battle against the spiders long enough to come to my attention. I recruited all of the warriors in the band, then betrayed the position of the rest to the Visorak. I hate loose ends.

From the start, Primal was difficult. He refused any biomechanical implants, accepting only a small paralysis device implanted under his skin. Like Gatherer, he collected trophies from his hunts. But after a short time, he started refusing to take missions that did not hold the promise of a good trophy. In addition, his fierce sense of justice occasionally led him to hunt one of our clients rather than the assigned target. For now, I tolerate him because he is extremely effective. But should I tire of his eccentricities, his existence will come to an abrupt end.

POWERS: Primal uses his paralysis device only as a last resort. He prefers to rely on strength, speed, an uncanny knowledge of tactics, and his trusty spear.

STATUS: Active. Primal is one of the few Dark Hunters who operates solely on his own. He objects to the attitudes and behavior of many of the other Hunters, and tends to express his displeasure with his spear.

DESIGNED BY PETER DOLAN

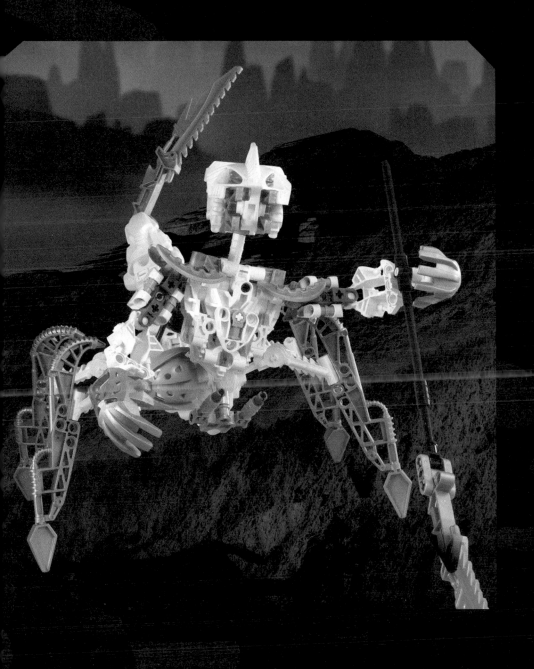

PROTOTYPE

Not every experiment works out the way you want it to. Take Prototype, for example. One of my Dark Hunters discovered a weapon he believed would be effective against Toa. To prove it, he tracked down a Toa of Fire and a Toa of Earth and blasted them just as they were merging their forms. But instead of destroying them, the weapon fused the two Toa together permanently and drove them mad. The result, Prototype, went on a rampage and then disappeared for several centuries.

He was discovered again by my agents, living in a swamp on an otherwise desolate island. In some strange way, his life force had become tied to his armor, and his armor was damaged. He was brought back to my island and restored to health. So many years alone had increased his madness, making it easy to sway him to my side.

Originally, we believed the new weapon we had discovered would help to rid us of Toa. Instead, it resulted in a new recruit to our cause. Unstable, yes; violent, unquestionably; insane, without a doubt. But those are just the sort of qualities I look for in a Dark Hunter.

POWERS: Prototype still retains some elemental power over fire and earth. Over time, his organic parts have become almost nonexistent, making him virtually all machine. Although slow-moving, he is extremely strong and almost invulnerable. After so many years, it would take an enormous amount of force to even scratch his armor, let alone damage it.

STATUS: Active. When he is not on missions, Prototype serves as a practice target for other Dark Hunters. If they survive their encounter with him, they are ready to face the world.

DESIGNED BY ALEX MUNROE

RAVAGER

It was a happy day indeed when the being now code-named Ravager was brought to the shores of my island. True, he did escape his handlers and proceed to destroy roughly one-third of the base. But did I order him dismembered on the spot? No. I suppose I am just soft-hearted.

What is it that makes Ravager such a charming sort? Is it his stinger tail, whose venom burns like the bites of a million fireflyers? His ruthless skill with sword and shield? Or is it that he has never seen two bricks together that he did not want to blow apart, or a living thing that he did not feel would be better off dead?

My Dark Hunters found Ravager wandering on a rocky coastline, with apparently no memory of where he came from or who he was. I have pressed him — *hard* — to try and remember. Imagine an entire army of such beings under my banner!

POWERS: In addition to enormous strength, Ravager possesses a sword and shield that seem almost capable of conscious thought. They automatically increase in strength to match any foe or obstacle they encounter.

STATUS: Active, always. It became obvious early that Ravager reacted to inactivity by destroying his surroundings. Thus I do not allow him back onto the island, but keep him constantly on missions.

DESIGNED BY JASON STROUD

REIDAK

Reidak likes to break things — big things, small things, living things, it makes no difference to him. That, plus his impatient, emotional nature, leads some to believe he is as dumb as he is big. That is a mistake. Part of Reidak's appeal to my organization was that he combined raw power with intelligence and cunning.

My agents found Reidak alone on his home island. According to their report, there had once been a thriving civilization there. All that changed when Reidak had a minor argument with an order enforcement officer. That escalated into a series of disputes with local officials. There followed a screaming match with the city overseer, and before it was all over, there weren't two stones still together in the city. Those who did not flee the island suffered the inevitable fate of the slow-moving.

After joining the Dark Hunters, Reidak carried out a number of "smash and grab" missions, with emphasis on the "smash." He exhibited an unwillingness to plan, a lack of respect for the concept of stealth, and an intense dislike of enclosed places (like cells). Why he chose to defy my orders, go treasure hunting, and end up as a Piraka, I do not know. But once he has been captured, I am sure I will think of some way to get the answers I want.

POWERS: In addition to his great strength, Reidak has the unusual ability to adapt after every defeat, making it impossible to beat him the same way twice. He also possesses infrared and thermal imaging vision.

STATUS: Rogue. Reidak is currently with the other Piraka on the island of Voya Nui, a place so dangerous that even Dark Hunters prefer to avoid it. But he has to leave sometime. . . .

SAVAGE

Savage was a Toa who had the misfortune to encounter a scouting patrol of Visorak. At that time, little was known in the universe at large about the spiderlike creatures and what they could do. Savage was captured and transformed into a Toa Hordika, but the rest of his team escaped.

When Savage finally freed himself and made his way back to his comrades, none of them recognized him. They attacked, believing him to be a monster. As his rage and despair grew, the transformation accelerated, until he lost the ability to speak and could only growl and bellow. Losing control, he badly hurt his former friends. Then he fled, his mind filled with grief, guilt, and anger.

Give me a flicker of rage, and I can fan it into an inferno. When I had him in hand and learned from my spies what had happened to him, I convinced him that the others on his team had been jealous. They had allowed him to be trapped and turned into a beast. In his maddened state, he was ready to believe friends were enemies — and I had a new Dark Hunter.

POWERS: Savage is a skilled hunter, able to track a mote of dust across a desert. His Rhotuka spinner can paralyze his enemies, and his tri-claw has the power to liquefy solid matter.

STATUS: Temporarily inactive. Every now and then, Savage is seized by madness and has to be restrained so as not to harm himself or other Dark Hunters. Right now, he is in a specially prepared cell in my fortress. When he calms down, he will be released. His pay will be docked for the extensive damage he has caused to the cell walls and door.

DESIGNED BY C. J. KONOPKA

SEEKER

It is not unusual to have someone join the Dark Hunters in furtherance of their own aims and ambitions. Seeker is one such being, and only time will tell if he makes the unwise decision to try and quit after he achieves his goal.

Seeker was originally a servant of the Brotherhood of Makuta and one of the guardians of the Kanohi Mask of Light (after the Brotherhood stole it from its makers, of course). His task, one at which he failed miserably, was to keep it safe. The Toa Hagah stole the mask and escaped, though not before being transformed into bestial Rahaga. Seeker was cast out of the Brotherhood and began a personal mission of vengeance, searching for the Rahaga with the intent of getting the mask back.

To date, he has not done so. The Rahaga turned the mask over to the Toa Metru, who took it out of Metru Nui. It would seem the Rahaga would have been easy targets at that point, since they were staying in the city — and so they would have been, if I had allowed Seeker to find out that information. As I said, it would be a shame if he achieved his goal, decided to resign, and I had to kill him. So instead, he continues to carry out missions for me, unaware of how close he is to those he has sought for so long.

POWERS: Seeker's primary weapon is his staff, which can both weaken an opponent physically and deliver seismic shocks. When done in that sequence, the earth tremor delivers an incredibly powerful blow to an already-dazed foe.

STATUS: Active. Seeker is always eager for new missions that take him to places he has not been before. He hopes that on one of these journeys, he will find the Rahaga. Needless to say, he is never assigned tasks on Metru Nui.

DESIGNED BY DANIEL WALSH

SENTRAKH

My most loyal servant, Sentrakh is the one being in all the universe I believe I can trust. His past is a mystery, not only to the other Dark Hunters, but to himself. All he knows is that he must follow my lead and act on my will — his life has no other purpose. Would he be so eager to obey, I wonder, if he knew I was responsible for turning him into what he is?

Sentrakh is not living, nor is he dead. He inhabits a sort of shadow state between the two, the result of certain . . . experiments I once attempted in an effort to create more loyal and obedient Dark Hunters. I was successful, but in the process, his memory was erased. The time spent reeducating him made future use of this process ill-advised.

I can truly say that I owe Sentrakh my life. It was he who saved me after my battle with Makuta, so many years ago. He got me to my island, where I could take the time to recover my health and nurse my rage. Perhaps someday, if I am feeling charitable, I will free him from his current empty existence . . . and repay his gift of life with my gift of death.

POWERS: Sentrakh possesses the natural powers of illusion casting, darkness, molecular transmutation, and mind wipe. He can also launch a Rhotuka spinner that causes its target to temporarily dematerialize.

STATUS: Active. Sentrakh is currently hunting the Piraka. He has orders to capture them or, if they prove sufficiently annoying, to eliminate them.

SHADOW STEALER

A most unusual being, Shadow Stealer is a Dark Hunter who hates other Dark Hunters. Legends about him abound, but actual facts are in short supply. Still, he has proven most useful, eliminating the less efficient members of my organization. I think of him as a plague, striking the weak and making the strong even stronger.

He is ancient, perhaps even older than I. Some whisper that he was a hero long before the first Toa ever appeared in the universe, possibly a crusader of a completely different type. Eventually, his time passed, and Toa became the chosen warriors of Mata Nui. Perhaps he resented that, perhaps he simply could find no place in this new world . . . but he turned to the Dark Hunters.

I initially dispatched him to the farthest reaches of the universe on a mission that should have taken years to complete. He finished his task in days and has been working his way back to my island ever since, defeating Toa and Dark Hunters as he goes. Eventually, he will reach my very gate, and he and I will find out which of us is truly the stronger.

POWERS: Shadow Stealer is able to absorb the shadows that surround him and convert them into energy. He can also slip into shadow and reemerge in a place of his choosing, provided there is a shadow there for him to enter and exit. Apparently, there is a range limit to this ability or he would have returned by now . . . unless he is simply sharpening his claws for our eventual confrontation.

STATUS: Active. Shadow Stealer's powers make him uniquely well suited to battle the Brotherhood of Makuta. I have actually heard a rumor that the Brotherhood attempted to hire another Dark Hunter to eliminate him!

DESIGNED BY AARON CASSITY

SPINNER

Sometimes, the most fertile ground for recruiting Dark Hunters is among our enemies, the Toa. Nidhiki was not the only, or even the first, Toa to join my organization, although he was more reluctant than most. The Dark Hunter known as Spinner, for example, was positively eager to defect.

His story is a familiar one. A member of a contentious team of Toa locked in battle with mutated Rahkshi, Spinner was hurled into a near-bottomless pit during the fight. He claims it was one of the other Toa who did it, though it could just as easily have been a Rahkshi. When my agents found him, he was broken and battered and close to death.

We returned him to health and made some . . . improvements. Although he lost access to his elemental air power, he remains an effective Dark Hunter to this day. Unfortunately, he is of little use on stealth missions. The process used on him resulted in the air around him turning heavy and poisonous. It has remained that way.

POWERS: Spinner's eyes can cause vertigo in his target with just a glance. His twin slicers launch Rhotuka that affect an enemy's sense of balance. If the slicers are combined, the resulting Rhotuka can plunge a foe into a coma (although the amount of energy needed to create this Rhotuka incapacitates Spinner for some time as well).

STATUS: Active. Since his powers work well over distance, he can disable perimeter guards around a target very quietly and efficiently. He says he only wants to hunt Toa, but I have insisted that he take the missions given to him or else we will see how he likes being the focus of his own power . . . permanently.

DESIGNED BY JOSHUA GUTHRIE

SUBTERRANEAN

The Dark Hunter I call Subterranean was an Onu-Matoran on Metru Nui many, many years ago. During the Toa–Dark Hunter war in that city, he was helping to build a new wing of the Archives beneath Ga-Metru when the tunnel ceiling collapsed. Exactly what happened next is unclear — it is possible that there was some experiment going on in the building above, the contents of which spilled on him. Regardless, he mutated over the course of time into the bizarre and frightening figure we now know.

When Subterranean finally emerged, he found that his appearance terrified his former friends. Shocked and grief-stricken, he left the city with the Dark Hunters at the conclusion of the war. Since that time, he has served me and has proved to be a most effective hunter of Toa.

Unfortunately, the accident that created Subterranean had one major side effect: His sense of hearing was increased to the point that the slightest sound is actually painful to him. Therefore, he has been fitted with special armor that dampens sound. Needless to say, he attempts to avoid Toa of Sonics as much as possible.

POWERS: Subterranean is capable of disassembling any object with just a touch, making him an excellent saboteur. He is also able to temporarily immobilize enemies with his glance.

STATUS: Active. Most recently, I dispatched Subterranean to meet with a tribe of Frostelus to discuss an alliance, on the theory that he is one of the few beings uglier than they are.

DESIGNED BY PAUL FISCHER

THOK

Thok's unique talents were first discovered when he actually dared attempt to steal from the Dark Hunters. Three of my agents were on a mission near a Brotherhood of Makuta fortress when Thok froze them and tried to get away with their weapons. He failed, of course, but rather than execute him, my Hunters brought him to me.

I discovered quickly that he was brilliant, arrogant, and did not work well with others. Part of the reason for this was that he had a tendency to abandon his companions to their fate when things went wrong. He was also a bit too good at exploiting the conflicts between his teammates and turning them against each other to his own advantage.

He did turn out to be an excellent hunter of Toa. He would not hesitate to sacrifice everyone else on his team in order to get his target. I was not surprised when he betrayed the Dark Hunters and became a Piraka in a quest for power — I will, however, be surprised if he survives the experience.

POWERS: Thok has the power to bring any inanimate object to life and make it serve him, from a rock to a tree to a piece of equipment. He has a natural immunity to extreme cold, and his ice weapon allows him to freeze others instantly. His spellbinder vision can disorient a target long enough for capture. Extreme heat weakens Thok. And he can be driven slightly mad by having to spend too much time around others.

STATUS: Rogue. Thok is with his fellow Piraka on the island of Voya Nui, seeking the Mask of Life. If he is fortunate, he will perish there. If he is not, he will fall into my hands again.

TRACKER

Tracker's story is a complex one, for his accounts of his origin vary from time to time. One day, he blames Visorak venom for making him what he is; another day it is Roodaka's mutation spinner that was the cause. Whatever the case may be, he has a deep hatred of the Visorak branch of the Brotherhood of Makuta's army, and that is an emotion I have been able to put to use.

As his name implies, Tracker and his pet bull are skilled at hunting down targets. Give him the slightest scent or even an object once handled by his quarry, and Tracker will find the unfortunate being no matter where it tries to hide.

Perhaps Tracker's most impressive accomplishment was tracking down Roodaka after her supposed death in Metru Nui. It required three other Dark Hunters to prevent him from killing her, but eventually she was "persuaded" to come to my island for a discussion about her future.

POWERS: In addition to his skills mentioned above, Tracker possesses tremendous strength. The horns of his pet bull are capable of dissolving solid matter upon contact.

STATUS: Active. Tracker is now employed seeking out a renegade Brotherhood of Makuta member who is in hiding from both his former comrades and the Dark Hunters.

DESIGNED BY AUSTIN ALLEN

TYRANT

This Dark Hunter was the only real challenge to my rule
prior to the rebellion of the Piraka. Before joining my
organization, Tyrant was the brutal ruler of a small island to
the south. His subjects lived in mortal fear of him, and well
they should have, considering that finding new and better
ways to perform executions was his favorite hobby.

He agreed to ally with the Dark Hunters during our war with
the Toa, but I do not think Tyrant ever fully considered
himself a member. He spent most of the conflict trying to
undermine my authority and take control himself. So I gave
him the opportunity to prove his bravery, sending him with a
small patrol of Hunters to confront Toa Lhikan and a band
of Toa.

Of course, I had neglected to tell him that the Dark Hunters
he traveled with had orders to abandon him the second the
fight was joined. Tyrant was demolished by the Toa and
disappeared beneath the waves of the silver sea. It is my
understanding that he vowed vengeance upon both myself
and the Toa before vanishing. It is possible he may one day
return to keep that vow, but I am not waiting up.

POWERS: Tyrant had the ability to absorb heat, causing his
entire body to reach dangerously high temperatures and
giving his armor a fiery red color. He could release a massive
heat blast and also use superheated air to levitate. He was
impervious to both extreme heat and extreme cold.

STATUS: Unknown. No one has seen Tyrant since he
disappeared in the ocean. No one has missed him, either.

DESIGNED BY ERIC RICHTER

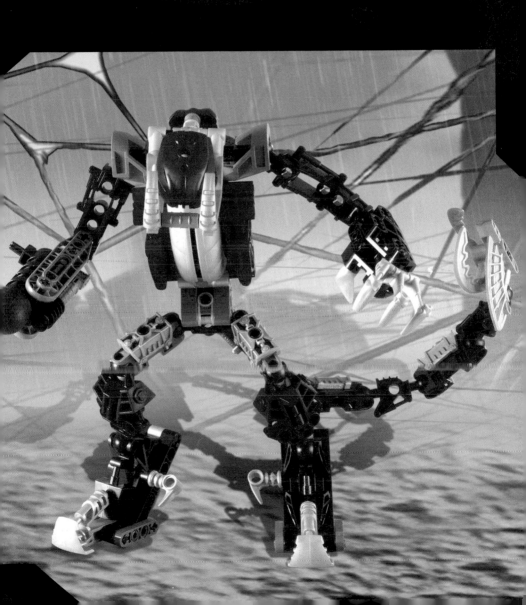

VANISHER

Some Dark Hunters are blindly loyal, sufficiently effective to remain employed, and perfectly willing to follow orders as long as they get paid and get the chance to kill something now and then. And then there are those like Vanisher.

Independent, powerful, and with a nasty habit of disobeying orders, Vanisher would have been executed long ago if he were not so successful. Not that he would be easy to catch — he can, after all, appear and disappear at will. As I did with Nidhiki, I tried partnering Vanisher with more faithful Dark Hunters who would keep him in line. Somehow, they all wound up "accidentally" dying on their joint missions with him.

Lately, I have begun to suspect that Vanisher may be working for the Brotherhood of Makuta as well as for me. I am pondering how best to use that knowledge to my advantage.

POWERS: Vanisher's power may rest in his weapon or in him — he refuses to say. His spear is capable of opening dimensional gates through which he can step, allowing him to travel vast distances in the blink of an eye. To an outsider, it appears that he has just disappeared. He is also able to open pocket dimensions to capture energies hurled against him. He can keep the energies there until he chooses to release them at a target. More than once, he has defeated an enemy by using nothing but his opponent's own power.

STATUS: Active. I have dispatched him to the nearest fortress of the Brotherhood of Makuta to gather intelligence. I have sent another Dark Hunter to spy on him, and yet a third to spy on both. If he has betrayed us, I will know about it.

DESIGNED BY JOHNATHAN MASTRON

VEZOK

Nasty and vicious . . . everything one could ask for in a Dark Hunter. On the outside, Vezok always seemed like a calm, cool, and efficient operative. But on the inside, he was an explosion waiting to happen. Stay on his good side, and all would be well — unfortunately, his good side was so narrow, it was almost invisible. Get on his bad side, and he would wreck you, your home, your village, and your continent — just for his own amusement.

Why Vezok ended up with the Piraka is something of a mystery, as he cannot stand Hakann, Zaktan, or the others. Reidak is the only one he can tolerate, and only because he doesn't consider Reidak smart enough to plot against him. Still, he chose ambition over loyalty, and there is a price to be paid for that.

Prior to turning traitor, Vezok's last mission as a Dark Hunter involved three Turaga and an ancient tablet of some value. I know the mission was successful, but he never returned with the tablet, meaning it must be hidden somewhere. Finding the talent matters at least slightly more to me than punishing Vezok for his disobedience, so we may have to strike a bargain.

POWERS: Vezok is capable of absorbing the powers of those in close proximity to him, storing them, and then using them himself. He also possesses powerful impact vision. His harpoon can propel him rapidly through the water, and his buzz saw hurls water daggers. He reportedly also carries a zamor sphere launcher.

STATUS: Rogue. No doubt he will prove a great asset to his new team . . . unless, of course, they get him angry.

ZAKTAN

Zaktan is a mystery I would like to solve . . . preferably slowly and with the maximum amount of pain for him. As the self-styled leader of the Piraka, he represents a threat to my authority that must be destroyed.

I recruited Zaktan personally. He was working as a slave in a protodermis mine when I first encountered him. I could see the hatred in his eyes, the contempt for concepts like honor and trust, and I knew I could mold him into a fearsome Dark Hunter. I oversaw his training and taught him to lie, manipulate, and strike without warning. Then I assigned him to lead a team devoted to capturing and eliminating Toa.

Unfortunately, Zaktan grew ambitious. When he dared to defy me, I blasted him with my devastating eyebeams. But he did not die — instead, his body was shattered into billions of pieces, each one containing a portion of his consciousness. He could control each microscopic piece at will, making him even more powerful than before. Whether he was always made up of so many tiny creatures (called protodites), or whether my beams somehow altered him, I do not know. Someday, I hope for the chance to dissect him and find out.

POWERS: In addition to being able to control the shape of his body, Zaktan is capable of dispersing into a cloud of protodites to avoid being struck, he can fly, and he can regenerate parts of himself that are destroyed. He also possesses laser vision. Zaktan carries a three-bladed sword and a zamor sphere launcher.

STATUS: Rogue. My spies report Zaktan is with the other Piraka on the island of Voya Nui. I will be waiting when he leaves there.

BIONICLE

FIND THE POWER,
LIVE THE LEGEND

The legend comes alive in these exciting BIONICLE® books:

BIONICLE Chronicles
#1 Tale of the Toa
#2 Beware the Bohrok
#3 Makuta's Revenge
#4 Tales of the Masks

The Official Guide to BIONICLE
BIONICLE Collector's Sticker Book
BIONICLE Mask of Light
BIONICLE Encyclopedia
BIONICLE Rahi Beasts

BIONICLE Adventures
#1 Mystery of Metru Nui
#2 Trial by Fire
#3 The Darkness Below
#4 Legends of Metru Nui
#5 Voyage of Fear
#6 Maze of Shadows
#7 Web of the Visorak
#8 Challenge of the Hordika
#9 Web of Shadows
#10 Time Trap